For my sister, Melissa:
the person with whom I first shared
the magic of Christmas
—D.B.H.

For my huge, loving,
Christmas-obsessed family
—J.P.

The illustrations in this book were made digitally on a tablet that was carried around everywhere.

Cataloging-in-Publication Data has been applied for and may be obtained from the Library of Congress.

ISBN 978-1-4197-6013-6

Text © 2023 Donna Barba Higuera
Illustrations © 2023 Juliana Perdomo
Book design by Heather Kelly

Printed and bound in China
10 9 8 7 6 5 4 3 2 1

Abrams Books for Young Readers are available at special discounts when purchased in quantity
for premiums and promotions as well as fundraising or educational use. Special editions can also be
created to specification. For details, contact specialsales@abramsbooks.com or the address below.

Abrams® is a registered trademark of Harry N. Abrams, Inc.

ABRAMS The Art of Books
195 Broadway, New York, NY 10007
abramsbooks.com

IT'S NAVIDAD, EL CUCUY!

STORY BY
DONNA BARBA
HIGUERA

PICTURES BY
JULIANA
PERDOMO

*El Cucuy: pronounced *el ku-koo-ee*

Abrams Books for Young Readers
New York

"¡Feliz Navidad, El Cucuy!"

"What are you doing to my perfect prickly pot?
I don't want any Happy Christmas!"

"These lights are too bright!" says El Cucuy.

"Los farolitos
will light your way
in the dark,"
Ramón explains.

"¡Exactamente! I love the dark. This is horrible!"

"Oh, El Cucuy—if you will not come to Navidad,
then Christmas will come to you."

"¡Mira! Isn't it magical?" Ramón asks.

El Cucuy gasps.

"¡Ay! A monster!"

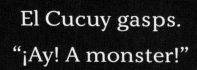

"It's only a new tradition in our new home,
El Cucuy," Ramón says. "Un muñeco de nieve."

"A man made of snow?"

"¡Sí! Should we give him a name?"

"Why give him a name?" El Cucuy huffs.
"He is not real."

"He is real if we believe he is real."

"Hmmpphh!"

"Who are those strangers?" El Cucuy asks.

"They are not strangers," Ramón answers. "Tonight, we will welcome those who were once strangers but are now family. They followed la estrella to our casa."

El Cucuy jumps back. "Oh, no! How can we stop them?"

"Silly El Cucuy! It's Nochebuena, the final day of Las Posadas.
They have knocked on many doors for nine nights. At each door,
they sing a song, asking for a safe place to eat and sleep.
But no one has let them in."

"¡Oh, qué bueno! So, they are not coming here either!"

Ramón sighs. "Can you imagine how hard it would be?
To have walked so far and for so long, only to have
door after door shut in your face?"

El Cucuy drops his head. "That *would* feel terrible."

"But our casa will be different," Ramón says.
"It will be the final house on the final night. When they
arrive here, they will sing, and we will welcome them in.

The last casa is a
reminder of what we
should all do. When
someone is lost or
hungry or needs help . . .

Knock!
Knock!
Knock!

. . . we treat them with kindness."

"What is that delicious smell?"

Ramón sniffs deeply. "I think it's the tamales.
But you're a cucuy, so maybe your monster
nose likes the smell of pozole or buñuelos.
Oh, or el ponche!"

"What is this
magical drink?"

"It's horchata.
And sí, it is mágica!"

CRACK!

"¡Dios mío! What is that noise?"

Ramón laughs. "The piñata.
Come on. It's our turn!"

"Why should I join you?"

Ramón hugs El Cucuy.
"Because it is what families do.
We celebrate together."

"I am your family?"

"Por supuesto."

"Toma, El Cucuy, I brought you un regalo."

"¿Qué es?"

¡FELIZ NAVIDAD, EL CUCUY!

"Bienvenido, Ramón. Just like you
welcomed your neighbors into our home,
I am welcoming you to my pot!"

"I know this may seem odd to you,
but this is what we do on Navidad.

We welcome those who were once
strangers but are now family.

And now that you are family,
you must have a name.
We shall call you Helado!"

AUTHOR'S NOTE

Las Posadas, meaning "the inn," begins each year on December 16, ending with Nochebuena on Christmas Eve on December 24. Every evening, families walk from home to home singing a song, "Las Posadas," asking for shelter. Each night, they are turned away. On the final night, Nochebuena, they make the same procession. But at the last home, when they sing "Las Posadas," all are welcomed inside. Everyone gathers in the final home to celebrate with delicious food: buñuelos, tamales, ponche, pozole, atole, café de olla, and even horchata. If you are careful and creep like a cucuy, you may be able to sneak treats off the tables while the grown-ups are busy with all the food and music and celebration.

But the treats don't end there! An important part of the evening is the breaking of the Posada piñata, which is filled with candy, nuts, or fruit. Just don't forget to share with El Cucuy, or he might jump up and down on your bed and keep you awake!

ILLUSTRATOR'S NOTE

In Colombia, we have something similar to the Posadas: We call them las Novenas. During the nine days before Christmas, we gather in different family homes, read the novena, sing villancicos, and eat traditional food. I have beautiful, heartwarming memories of tables full of buñuelos and natilla, crowded living rooms, my dad and Uncle Pepe playing their guitars, kids sitting on the floor with tambourines, and my grandpa singing as loud as he could. We honor our ancestors through music with love and joy.